BROBARIANS

LINDSAY WARD

two lions

For Frank and Jackson,
my two best guys, always and always

Text and illustrations copyright © 2017 by Lindsay Ward

Published by Two Lions, New York
www.apub.com

ISBN-13: 9781503941670 (hardcover)
ISBN-10: 1503941671 (hardcover)

The illustrations are rendered in cut paper, pencil, and crayon on chipboard.

Book design by Abby Dening
Printed in China

First Edition
1 3 5 7 9 10 8 6 4 2

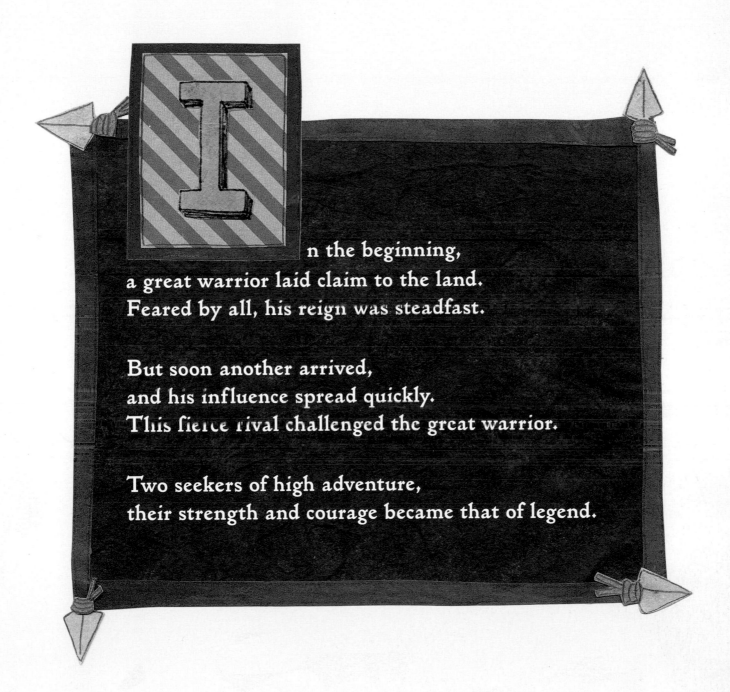

In the beginning,
a great warrior laid claim to the land.
Feared by all, his reign was steadfast.

But soon another arrived,
and his influence spread quickly.
This fierce rival challenged the great warrior.

Two seekers of high adventure,
their strength and courage became that of legend.

This is the tale of the mighty Brobarians...

TWO WARRIORS,

once at peace . . .

UH-OH

. . . were now at odds.

IGGY

THE

BROBARIAN

stood as tall as a giant,
with the strength of ten men.

A **master**
of the sword,

he **plundered** wondrous treasures,

conquered
magical beasts,

and **challenged**
colossal monsters.

Many sought his counsel.

Atop the dark mountain,
the great warrior looked on . . .

...as Iggy
seized his army!

He was not amused.

For it was he who had the strength of twenty men!
He who had defeated the scariest beasts!
He who'd plundered the most treasure!

(scary beast)

HE RULED ALL!

The great warrior called upon
his most trusted advisers

and waited for the perfect moment to strike. . . .

Later that day,
Iggy entered his cave
to feast and rest.

He paused, sensing a dark mischief was afoot....

"Bah-bah?"

Iggy's most prized possession was

Iggy's cry echoed across the land.

Iggy knew where he must go.

He **scaled** perilous mountains,

navigated
treacherous
quicksand,

and **battled** through
raging storms.

Finally, he reached the dark mountain.
His greatest foe emerged . . .

OTTO THE BIG BROBARIAN!

(dun-dun-dun...)

Iggy raised his sword high,
challenging the great warrior.

Then Otto did the unthinkable . . .

...and guzzled Iggy's bah-bah,
finishing every drop!

Iggy would not yield
to this treachery.
A battle cry erupted. . . .

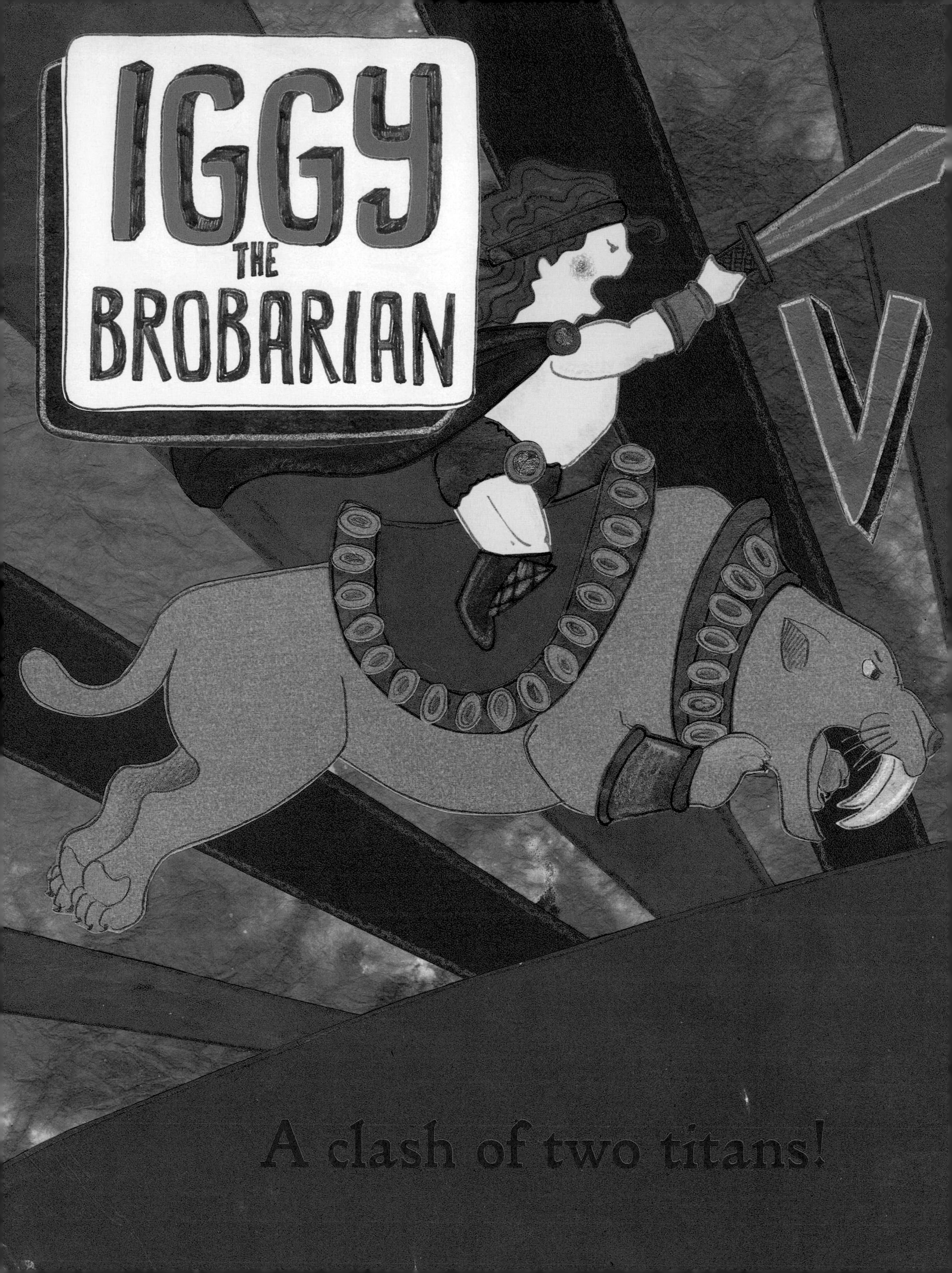
IGGY
THE
BROBARIAN
V
A clash of two titans!

OTTO
THE
BIG BROBARIAN

The sky grew dark
and menacing as
the battle raged on.

A path of destruction
ensued across the land.

Then they heard it,
summoning them from above—

a most powerful magic,

a magic that ruled all.

OTTO! IGGY!

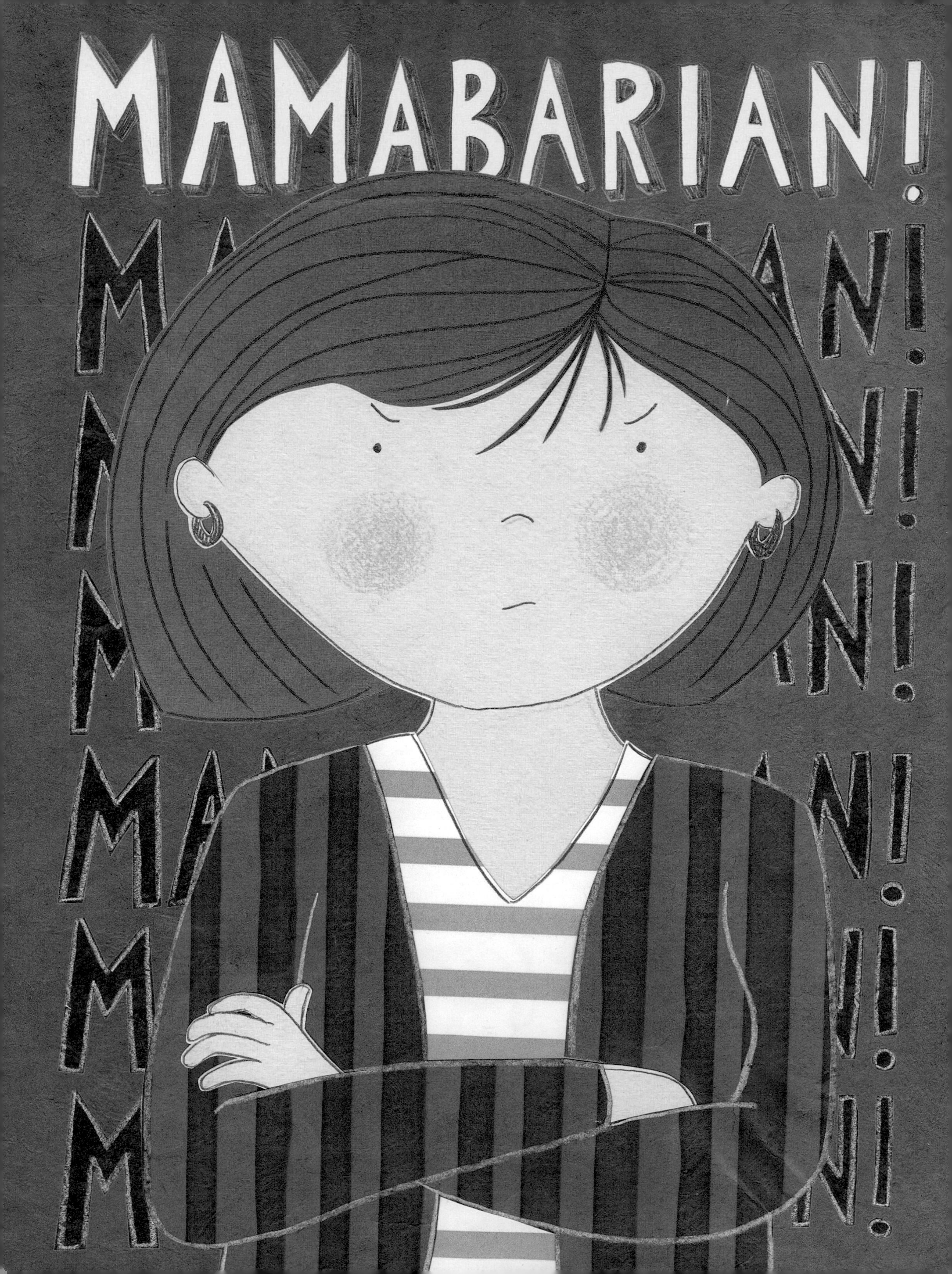
MAMABARIAN!

Iggy and Otto stood still,
dropping their swords
to the ground.

Heads bowed in shame,
they marched inside
to the dungeon of seclusion.

And so it was . . .

...the legendary tale of Iggy the Brobarian and Otto the Big Brobarian.

Warriors.

Gladiators.

BARBARIANS.

BROTHERS.

Who live to fight another day...